Witty Stories of
Akbar & Birbal

RIDHIMA SHARMA

Published by
NAMASKAR BOOKS
Building No. 2/42 (Second Floor)
Ansari Road, Daryaganj
New Delhi-110002
e-mail: namaskarbooks@gmail.com
Website: www.namaskarbooks.com

ISBN 978-93-5521-776-9
WITTY STORIES OF AKBAR & BIRBAL
by Ridhima Sharma

Edition
First, 2023

Price
₹ 350 (Rupees Three Hundred Fifty Only)

Printed at
Japan Art, Delhi

Author's Note

The stories of Akbar and Birbal don't need any introduction as they are widely known. The friendship between Emperor Akbar and his favourite minister Birbal is an example of the most-strangest, yet a strong friendship. The duo is famous for their teasing banter and they often indulged in humourous exchanges.

For those who don't know who Emperor Akbar and Birbal were: Akbar was the third Mughal ruler who ruled India from 1556 to 1605. He was a powerful leader and a successful general who was responsible for the expansion of the Mughal Empire to most of the Indian subcontinents. It was during his reign that the Mughal Empire tripled in size, power and wealth.

He had nine extraordinary officials in his court whom he called "Navaratna". One of these "Navaratnas" was his Foreign Minister and good friend, Birbal. Birbal was famous for his quick wit and good sense of humour. He was the only Hindu Navaratna in Emperor Akbar's court. His real name was Mahesh Das.

With the means of these witty tales of Akbar and Birbal, you could teach your children the importance of wisdom and common sense. Also, through these stories, one can learn how to deal with difficult situations without losing one's composure and wit. Here, you will learn how you can turn even the most unfavourable situation in your favour by using wisdom and wit. Moreover, you will learn how wisdom, common sense and a good sense of humour could help you gain respect everywhere in the world. They also could get you out of the most difficult situations.

Hopefully, these witty stories will help the reader to get a good laugh and learn some valuable life lessons.

– Ridhima Sharma

Contents

1.

Back to Square One

As usual, a lot of people were present in Akbar's durbar.

A famous astrologer had come from a faraway country.

He was talking about the Solar System and the Earth's shape.

At one point, Akbar said, "If the earth is round, and if one travels straight towards one direction, he will come back to the same spot from where he has started the journey".

"Theoretically it is correct", said the astrologer.

"Why not in real life?", asked the king.

"One has to cross oceans, mountains and forests to keep the path straight", the astrologer said.

"Sail through the oceans, make tunnels in the mountains and use elephants to cross the forests". Akbar found the solution.

"Still it is impossible," said the astrologer.

"Why?" asked Akbar.

"It may take years to complete the whole journey," said the astrologer.

"Years? How many?" asked Akbar.

"I don't know. Maybe a hundred years or more", said the astrologer.

"Don't worry I will ask my ministers. They have an answer for everything". Akbar looked at his ministers.

"Impossible to calculate".

"Around 25 years".

"Fifty years or less".

"80 days".

"Why Birbal, you haven't uttered a word", the king showed his surprise at Birbal's silence.

"I was just calculating the time required to go round the earth", explained Birbal.

"And did you get the answer?" asked the king.

"Sure", said Birbal. "It will take just one day".

"Just one day! Birbal it is Impossible! Even it will take more than one day to cross our country", said Akbar.

"It is possible. Provided you travel at the speed of the Sun", said Birbal with a smile.

❑

2.

Full Moon, Quarter Moon

Once, Birbal went to Persia at the invitation of that country's king. Parties were extended in his honour and expensive gifts were heaped near him. On the eve of his departure to home, a nobleman asked him as to how he would compare the king of Persia with his King. Birbal said, "Your King is the full Moon, whereas mine is like a quarter Moon". The Persians were very happy to hear this analogy.

Now Birbal got home and he found that Emperor Akbar was furious with him. He demanded angrily, "How could you belittle your king? You are a traitor". Birbal said politely, "No, Your Majesty, no. I cannot belittle you. What I said there meant—"The Full Moon diminishes and disappears onward, while the quartered Moon grows gradually day by day. What I wanted to tell the world is that your power is growing day by day while the King of Persia's is about to decline now".

Akbar grunted in satisfaction and welcomed Birbal back from his journey with a warm embrace.

❑

3.

The Choice

One day, Emperor Akbar asked Birbal what he would choose if he were given a choice between justice and a gold coin.

"The gold coin," said Birbal. Akbar was taken aback.

"You would prefer a gold coin over justice?" he asked incredulously.

"Yes Jahanpanah," said Birbal.

The other courtiers were also amazed by Birbal's display of idiocy. For years they had been trying to discredit Birbal in the emperor's eyes without success but now the man had gone and done it himself. They could not believe their good fortune.

"I would have been dismayed if even the lowliest of my servants had said this," said the emperor. "But coming from you? It's... it's shocking and sad. I did not know you were so debased!"

"One asks only for what one does not have, Your Majesty," said Birbal quietly. "You have seen to it that in our country justice is available to everybody. So as the justice is already available to me too and as I'm always short of money, I said I would choose the gold coin".

The emperor was so pleased with Birbal's reply that he gave him not only one but a thousand gold coins.

❑

4.

Neither Here, Nor There

The wisdom of Birbal was unparalleled during the reign of Emperor Akbar. But Akbar's brother-in-law was extremely jealous of him. He asked the emperor to dispense him with Birbal's duties and appoint him in his place. He gave the emperor ample assurance that he would prove to be more efficient and capable than Birbal. Before Akbar could decide on this matter, this news reached Birbal.

Birbal himself resigned and left. Akbar's brother-in-law was made the minister in place of Birbal.

Akbar decided to test his new minister. He gave three hundred gold coins to him and said, “Spend these gold coins in such a way that I get a hundred gold coins here in this life, a hundred gold coins in the other world and another hundred gold coins neither here nor there”.

Now the minister found the entire situation to be a maze of confusion and hopelessness. He spent many sleepless nights worrying over how he would get himself out of this mess. Thinking in circles was making him go crazy. Eventually, on the advice of his wife, he sought Birbal’s help. Birbal said, “Just give me the gold coins. I shall handle the rest”.

Akbar’s brother-in-law had no choice so he gave all the coins to Birbal. Birbal walked the streets of the city holding the bag of gold coins in his hand. He noticed a rich merchant celebrating his son’s wedding. Birbal gave a hundred gold coins to him and bowed courteously saying, “Emperor Akbar sends you his good wishes and blessings for the wedding of your son. Please accept the gift he has sent”. The merchant felt honoured that the king had sent a special messenger with such a precious gift. He honoured Birbal and gave him a large number of expensive gifts and a bag of gold coins as a return gift for the king.

Next, Birbal went to the area of the city where the poor people lived. There he bought food and clothing in exchange for a hundred gold coins and distributed them in the name of the emperor.

When he came back to town, he organized a concert of music and dance. He spent a hundred gold coins on it.

The next day Birbal entered Akbar's court and announced that he had done all that the king had asked his brother-in-law to do. The emperor waited to know how he had done it. Birbal repeated the sequences of all the events and then said, "The money I gave to the merchant for the wedding of his son – you have got back while you are living on this earth. The money I spent on buying food and clothing for the poor – you will get that in the other world. The money I spent on the musical concert – you will get that neither here nor there".

❑

5.

Birth to a Child

Once, somebody had a wound in the palace of the emperor. The royal Vaidya was called and he suggested that if the milk of an ox's is applied on the wound, it will be cured soon. The emperor announced it in his court that he needed ox's milk. Everybody was surprised to hear this but they could not say anything.

A couple of days passed but nobody could find ox's milk. So Birbal was assigned this work. Birbal tried his best to explain to the emperor that there is no such thing as ox's milk, but he said, "When Raj Vaidya has asked for it, then it must exist. Bring it from anywhere". Birbal got very upset. He went home and thought about how to tell the emperor that there is no such thing like ox's milk.

Thinking about this, a couple of days passed and Birbal did not go to the court also. Akbar got worried about what has happened to Birbal? He sent somebody to his house to see why he did not come to the court. When the servant went there, he met Birbal's daughter washing his clothes just outside the house. She greeted the servant. The servant asked her, "What happened, Birbal has not come to the court?" The daughter replied, "Last night father had a child". The servant could not digest this statement but he came back and told this to the emperor. The emperor also could not understand this, so he decided to go to Birbal's house and find out the truth.

Seeing the emperor coming, Birbal greeted him. The emperor asked him, "Birbal, What is this? Can a man give birth to a child?"

Birbal politely replied, "Huzoor, when an ox can give milk, why can't a man give birth to a child?"

The Emperor understood that he was wrong. He returned to his palace and cancelled his order.

❑

6.

Generosity

One day a man stopped Birbal on a street and began narrating his woes to him. He finally said, "I have walked 20 miles to see you, and all along the way people kept saying that you are the most generous man in the country".

Birbal knew that the man is going to ask for some money from him. He asked, "Are you going back the same way?" The man replied, "Yes Sir". Birbal said, "Will you do me a favour?" The man said, "Certainly, why not? What do you want me to do?"

Birbal said, "Please deny the rumour of my generosity back to your home". And Birbal walked away.

❑

7.

How Birbal Brought Meat Back in the Community?

Akbar was famous for his religious tolerance. He would help all those who wanted help, even on religious matters.

Once, it so happened that a group of Brahmins appeared in his court and said, "O Great Emperor, You are the one who allowed us to ask you if we had problems. We have stayed silent for a long time, but today we wish to speak up. We do not want any slaughtering of animals, it is against our religion".

Hearing this Akbar was in a fix as the meat was the most important food in the market. He couldn't think of anything else except to call Birbal and ask his help in this matter. After thinking for a while, Birbal offered his solution. He said, "Your request can be granted on two conditions; one, that if any animal was found on the road, we are not responsible for his safety; two, that all animals should be fed in houses till their death. If any animal was found eating something outside, we are not responsible for his safety too".

Brahmins went back happily. A month went by. The same Brahmins again appeared in the court and said, "O Jahanpanah, we take our words back, we cannot keep our animals inside".

That is how Birbal brought meat back in the community.

❑

8.

Colourful Bird

Akbar was very fond of birds. One day a bird-catcher came to his kingdom. He had a very colourful bird. The bird-catcher said to Emperor Akbar that this bird is not only colourful like a peacock, but it can also dance and fly like him. The bird-catcher was immediately rewarded with 50 gold coins. He left the kingdom in a hurry.

When the bird catcher was gone, Birbal said to Emperor, "This bird cannot dance like a peacock and it has not bathed for many months". Birbal further suggested, "Let me give it a bath". He asked for a glass of water.

When Birbal gave the bath to the bird, everybody was surprised to see that it was not any special bird but a pigeon and the bird-catcher had fooled everybody by painting it. Its colour was coming out in the water.

Everybody asked Birbal that how did he know this. Birbal told that he saw colours on the nails of the bird-catcher. The bird-catcher was caught and given a punishment. The reward that was given to the bird-catcher was now given to Birbal.

❑

9.

Washerman's Donkey

Once, Akbar went to the river with his two sons and his wise minister, Birbal. On the bank of the river, Akbar and his two sons took off their clothes and asked Birbal to take care of them while they took bath in the river.

Birbal was waiting for them to come out of the river. All the clothes were on his shoulder. Looking at Birbal standing like this, Akbar felt like teasing him, so he said to him, "Birbal, you look like as if you are carrying a washerman's donkey's load".

Birbal quickly retorted, "Sir, Washerman's donkey carries only one donkey's load, while I am carrying three donkey's load". Akbar was speechless.

❑

10.

Hot Iron Test

One day, one man wanted to punish a man named Hasan. He accused him of stealing his necklace and reported this theft in the police. The case was brought in the judge's court. The judge knew Hasan very well, and he also knew that he was not a thief.

So he asked the man, "Why do you think that Hasan has stolen your necklace?" The man replied, "Your Honour, I have seen him stealing the necklace". Hasan said, "I am innocent, Your Honour. I do not know anything about his necklace".

The man then said, "All right, if he is innocent, let him prove his innocence. Let me bring the hot iron, and if he can hold it in his bare hands, then I will agree that he has not stolen my necklace and he is speaking the truth".

The man said, "It means that if I am speaking the truth, then I will not burn my hands with that red-hot iron?" "Yes, you are right. God will protect you".

Now Hasan could not do anything but to hold the red hot iron in his hands to prove his innocence, and that he was speaking the truth. He asked the judge to give him one day to look for that necklace again. The judge permitted him. He went home.

He took advice from Birbal. He returned the next day and said, "I am ready for that, sir. But if you think so, the same thing should apply to him too. If he is speaking the truth, then the red-hot iron should not burn his hands also. So let him bring that red hot iron holding in his both hands, then I will hold that iron in my bare hands".

Now the man was speechless. He told the judge that he would go and search for his necklace again in his house, maybe it was misplaced somewhere there. He bowed hastily and went away.

❑

11.

The Cock and the Hen

Since Birbal always outwitted Akbar, Akbar thought of a plan to make Birbal look like a fool. He gave one egg to each of his ministers before Birbal reached the court one morning.

So when Birbal arrived, the king narrated a dream he had the previous night saying that he would be able to judge the honesty of his ministers if they were able to bring back an egg from the royal garden pond.

So, Akbar asked all his courtiers to go to the pond, one at a time and return with an egg. So, one by one, all his ministers went to the pond and returned with the egg which he had previously given them.

Then it was Birbal's turn. He jumped into the pond and could find no eggs. He finally realized that the king was trying to play a trick on him. So he entered the court crowing like a cock.

The emperor asked him to stop making that irritating noise and then asked him for the egg.

Birbal smiled and replied that only hens lay eggs, and as he was a cock, he could not produce an egg.

Everyone laughed loudly and the king realized that Birbal could never be easily fooled.

❑

12.

The Hasty Judgement

Once, Emperor Akbar was riding near a mango grove. An arrow whizzed past him. His soldiers rushed to the grove and caught the person who did this. He was a young boy. On asking why did he wanted to kill the emperor, he said that he did not want to kill the emperor, he just wanted to knock down a mango from a high branch.

The emperor was too angry to listen to him. He ordered to put him to death in the same way as the boy had wanted to kill him.

A soldier tied the boy with a tree stump and steadied his arrow to kill him. Birbal, who was watching all this process quietly so far, now shouted, "This is not fair. If you want to shoot him in the same way as he tried to shoot the emperor, then you will have to aim for a mango. And then the arrow has to miss the mango and strike the boy".

Akbar had calmed down by now. Thinking that it was unfair to the boy, he ordered his soldiers to release the boy. Thus, Birbal saved that innocent boy.

❑

13.

Hunting and Dowry

Akbar had a passion for hunting. One day Akbar was on his hunting trip, when he heard two owls quarrelling very fiercely. Akbar asked Birbal, "Birbal, what are these owls saying? Why are they quarrelling so loudly?"

Birbal said, "Both of them are settling the dowry amount, Huzoor. The first one who is the groom's father is saying that he wants to take 40 jungles in the dowry, with no animals at all. The other owl, who is the bride's father is saying that he can arrange only 20 jungles at that moment".

In the meantime, one owl hooted once more very loudly. Akbar asked Birbal, "Now what is he saying?" Birbal said, "Now he is saying that if you wait for six months more, I can give you 40 jungles without animals".

Akbar understood what Birbal wanted to say—do not kill animals, so he gave up hunting altogether.

❑

14.

Fear is the Key

One day King Akbar said to Birbal, "Birbal, my people are very obedient to me. They love me very much". Birbal smiled and replied, "This is true, but they fear you too, Jahanpanah". Akbar could not agree on this, so it was decided that Birbal's statement should be tested.

Next day, according to Birbal's instructions, the king announced that he would be going for hunting, and people should pour a pot of milk in a tub kept in the courtyard. Next day when Akbar returned from hunting, he found that there was no milk in the tub, instead, there was only water. Akbar got very disappointed, but couldn't do anything.

Then Birbal said, "This time you will announce that you will come back and see the tub yourself". king did as Birbal said. Once again the tub was kept in the courtyard. This time when king returned from the hunting, he found the tub overflowing with milk. Birbal said, "I told you. It is your fear which made people obeys you. The first time there was no one to check the tub, so people poured the water, but the second time, they knew that you would check yourself that is why they brought the milk".

❑

15.

Footmark of an Elephant

Once, Emperor Akbar had a great quarrel with Birbal so Birbal left the place and went some 30 – 40 miles away in a village. There he started living hiding his identity.

Now Birbal's position (Deevaan or Minister) could not be kept empty so the king appointed his brother-in-law (wife's brother) in Birbal's place. Although Akbar didn't like this, he had to do this to please his wife. Very soon the city got undisciplined and complaints started coming to the king.

This was the time to test his brother-in-law's intelligence. So he went out to a Peer's Mazaar (the tomb of a saint). While returning from there he saw a footmark of an elephant. He asked his brother-in-law to protect that mark for three days. Badshah (Emperor) went to his palace and his brother-in-law started vigilance around it. The first day passed, the new Deevaan could not get any food; the second day also passed without any food. The third day he got very weak, but somehow survived. The fourth day he went to the king and told everything to him.

Badshah thought, "I have to call Birbal back, I can't do with this Deevaan". So he found a way to get him back. He announced that there is some quarrel over a government well so all Zameendaar (owner) of nearby villages should come to him with their wells, otherwise they will have to pay fine of 10,000 gold coins.

This order was heard in that village also in which Birbal lived. Its Zameendaar abused the king saying, "That this king has gone mad. Has anybody ever heard moving wells to other places? But if I did not go then I will have to pay 10,000 gold coins fine which is a lot of money".

When Birbal heard this, he knew that it was a trick to find him. He thought that now is the time to reveal his identity and keep the king's words. So he explained something to the Zameendaar and next day the Zameendaar along with Birbal and some of his servants arrived in Delhi. They did not enter the city, they stayed outside the city and sent a messenger to the king, "Huzoor, according to your orders we are here with our wells, now you send your wells to welcome them".

When Akbar heard this, he understood that Birbal was there. He asked the Zameendaar, "Who told this to tell me? Tell me the truth". The Zameendaar said, "Some time ago, a stranger came to stay in our village, he has asked us to tell you this". When asked about his form, he found it matched Birbal's. Then he sent his people to welcome Birbal and he was brought into the city with great pomp and show. Birbal was again appointed on his old position.

This time the emperor asked Birbal to protect that footmark of an elephant. Birbal said, "Done". He fixed an iron bar near the footmark and tied a 50-yard rope to it and told the villagers that whoever's house will fall inside the circumference of that rope his house will be demolished to protect that footmark".

People requested him not to do so and gave him gold coins as bribery for not to demolish their house. Thus, he collected approximately 100,000 gold coins. He deposited that money in the royal treasury and told the emperor that the work is done and 100,000 gold coins have been deposited in his treasury.

The king called his brother-in-law and said to him, "You were hungry for three days and gained nothing while protecting the footmark, but see, Birbal has earned 100,00 gold coins in one day only. That is why you can never be my Deevaan". The brother-in-law went away from there hanging his head down.

❑

16.

Heavy Burden

Once, a woman came to Birbal for his help. She said that the king wanted to construct some building on the land where her house was. She did not want to leave that place because that place belonged to her ancestors. Birbal assured her that she should be patient and he would try his best not to construct any building there.

Construction began. Now, one day, Birbal came to that site with King Akbar for inspection. He saw many gunny bags lying near the pile of mud. Birbal started filling the gunny bags with that mud. "Why are you doing this, Birbal?" asked the king. Birbal replied, "To earn merit for my next life".

Amused by this statement, Akbar also joined him. After Birbal had filled some bags, he requested Akbar to help him lift one of the gunny bags filled with mud.

"Oh, it is very heavy, Birbal," Akbar said lifting one bag.

Birbal said, "Think Huzoor, when only one bag is so heavy, how much mud will weigh in this piece of land and will it not weigh heavily on your conscience?"

Akbar realized his mistake and ordered to stop the construction on that site.

❑

17.

The Parrot Neither Eats, Nor Drinks

A person was very fond of parrots. He used to catch parrots, train them and sell them to interested people. One time he got a good parrot, so he trained him to talk, and when he was trained he presented him to the king. The king liked the parrot because he used to reply to his questions too.

The king made special arrangements for his safety, security and care and warned the people that if somebody will tell me about his death, he will be hanged. Hearing this, parrot was kept under very special care. But it so happened that one day the parrot suddenly died. Now, who should go and inform this to the king? Because whoever will inform the king about the death of the parrot, he will be sentenced to death. And who would like to die just for informing the king about the death of a parrot?

So the servant went to Birbal and told him about his plight. He said, "If I inform him about the parrot's death, then he will kill me, but if I do not tell him, then also he will kill me, so please save me".

Birbal thought for a while and sent him back to his work, and he went to the king and said, "Sir, Your parrot.."

The king asked, "What about the parrot?"

Birbal again stammered, "Your parrot, Sir".

The king asked, "Birbal, What happened to my parrot?"

Birbal again said, "Your parrot..".

The king asked, "I am asking you, what happened to my parrot? Say something about him in the name of Allaah".

Birbal said, "Jahanpanah, Your parrot neither eats anything, nor drinks water. Nor he speaks, moves his feathers, or opens his eyes.." The king said, "What? Has the parrot died?" Birbal said, "I did not say it. You said it".

King understood why Birbal had to say this in this way. He got very happy with Birbal's way of informing him about his parrot.

❑

18.

Whose Bag?

Once, it so happened that there was an oil merchant. When the villagers came to buy oil from him, he gave them the oil and collected money from them. One day he and a villager come to the court, both fighting for a bag of money. Each claimed that the bag belonged to him.

The merchant said that it was his bag when he turned to give the customer his oil, he pulled the bag from him and started fighting. The villager said that it was his bag when he was looking at some other things, he placed it in front of the merchant and the merchant started to claim it.

Everybody in the court was surprised and was waiting eagerly how Akbar would solve this problem.

Akbar asked Birbal to solve this case. Birbal asked a servant to get some water in a bowl. The servant brought the water. He then placed the bag in the bowl. After some time, everybody saw some oily substance floating on water. Birbal told that the bag belonged to the oil merchant not to the villager.

Everybody praised Birbal and the customer was punished.

❑

19.

Three Idols

As you know, Akbar considered Birbal the most intelligent person of his kingdom. Once, a sculptor challenged Badshah Akbar that he would show three idols to him, which would look exactly like each other to his courtiers and they would have to rate them good, ok and bad. Akbar agreed.

All the courtiers tried to rate them but failed because they were so alike that they did not know how to rate them. Now it was Birbal's turn. He noticed a small hole in the ears of the idols. Birbal got curious, so he took three wires and inserted them in those holes.

In the case of the first idol, the wire came out from the other ear. In the second idol's case, it came out of its mouth; but in the case of the third idol, it remained inside. He got the answer and he rated the third idol as good, the first idol ok and the second idol bad.

The sculptor could not understand what was the basis of rating the idols. He asked Birbal that how was he so sure? Birbal said, "The third idol (from whose ear the wire remained inside) did not tell others what somebody else had told it, that is why it was good. The first idol was OK (from whose ear the wire came out from the other ear) because it did not remember or tell others what somebody had told it. But the third idol (from whose ear the wire came out from the mouth) remembered everything and gave out the secret what was told to it to others.'

The sculptor was speechless and Akbar was very happy. He gave a big reward to Birbal.

❑

20.

Truth Always Finds Its Way

Once there was a religious man who wanted to go on a pilgrimage. He did not want to take his life's saving with him on his journey, so he went to one of his good friends and took him to a forest so that he could talk to him in private. There he told him that he was going on a pilgrimage and asked him to hold his savings for him till he comes back. He would collect it when he comes back. His friend agreed to keep his money for him and took the bag. The next day that man left for his pilgrimage.

Many years passed but the religious man did not return, but one fine morning that man came and knocked his friend's door and asked his money back. His friend kept changing the subject, but in the end, he had to say, "I don't know what are you talking about. What type of money are you talking about? The old man was shocked to hear this, but softly he reminded him of the whole incident. The friend said, "You are crazy. When did you give me the money? You are lying". The man kept requesting for his money but the friend did not hear a word and shut his door upon him.

The old man got very disappointed and went to Emperor Akbar. Akbar heard his story, called his wise advisor Birbal and handed over the case to him. Birbal also heard his story and called his friend to whom he gave his money. Birbal asked him to return the old man's money which he gave him before going on pilgrimage, but the friend refused saying that he did not give him any money.

Now Birbal got perplexed thinking what to do in this case. After a while, he asked the old man, "Do you have any witness that you gave your money to him?" "No, Sir. Because I gave him that money in a forest under a mango tree".

Birbal scolded him, "You are foolish to say that you have no witness. You do have a witness—that mango tree is your witness. Can't you get some help from that mango tree?" The old man kept looking at Birbal hearing this. How the hell that tree can help him in this matter? He kept thinking, is Birbal a fool? At the same time, Birbal said, "Go and bring that mango tree here. Tell him that Birbal wants you to be present before him in this case. Go quickly and bring it here".

The old man now was sure that Birbal had gone mad, but since he had no other alternative, he started towards the forest. Both Birbal and the friend sat waiting for the old man to bring the mango tree. One hour passed, two hours passed, when the old man did not come back, Birbal said loudly, "Why this man is not coming back, two hours have already passed. Why is he taking such a long time to do such a small task?"

The friend immediately spoke, "Sir, he can't possibly come so soon, because he would not have even reached that place yet". Birbal asked him, "What do you mean? Do you mean that that place is so far that it would take him more than two hours to reach there?" "Yes Sir, the place he told you is very far from here". Birbal said, "Oh, I see" and then kept quiet.

After a long time, the old man came and said to Birbal, "Sir, I gave your message to the tree but it did not answer". Birbal said, "Do not worry, the tree has already witnessed that you gave money to this man". Then he said to the old man's friend, "You have one more chance to accept your guilt and return the money to him". But the friend kept insisting that the old man did not gave any money to him.

Now Birbal asked, "Then how do you know that the tree under which he claimed that he gave the money to you, is so far from here?" After all this, the friend had to accept his lie and returned the money to the old man.

So remember, sooner or later the truth comes out in the light because to hide a truth we have to tell many lies and somewhere they clash and we are caught in them. While the truth is one, and it is easy to remember.

❑

21.

Greater than the God

Once a merchant came to Akbar's court and praised him a lot as he wanted Akbar to sign a trade agreement with a neighbouring country. He was praising him a lot as he wanted to impress him, but in a short while, he noticed that the emperor was not at all impressed with his praises. So he thought of another way to impress him. He shouted, "O Emperor, You are greater than even God", and sat quietly to notice the effect of his words.

Birbal was also listening to all this and was anticipating some kind of trouble out of this praise. So his brain started working ahead of time for its solution.

Akbar was very furious at the merchant's words. He was a very religious man and he did not like that somebody told him that he was greater than the God Himself who was the greatest of them all. But he liked the healthy discussions. He had got an opportunity to break a discussion on this issue, so he said to his courtiers, "Did you all hear this man saying that I am greater than the God Himself? If this is so, then tell me why is it so?" After having said this, he waited for the arguments of his courtiers regarding this statement.

Now how a king could be greater than God? His courtiers were silent in fear. This was a tricky question for them. Neither they could say 'Yes' nor could they say 'No'. One by one, they bent their heads down.

After a while, Akbar turned to his favourite Minister, Birbal and asked him, "Birbal, what do you say in this regard?" Birbal immediately said "He is right, Jahanpanah. You are greater than God". Akbar was stunned hearing this, he asked him again, "How Birbal, how is it possible that I am greater than God Himself. Explain to me. Are you trying to impress me with your lies?"

Birbal said, "No Huzoor, No. Why should I lie to you? You are indeed greater than God because there is one thing you can do but God can't".

"And what is that?" Akbar asked.

"God cannot banish anybody from His kingdom, because the whole Universe is His kingdom; but you can do it easily".

Akbar couldn't help bursting out laughing and said, "Birbal, you are the best, as always".

And he banished that merchant.

❑

22.

Master or Servant

Once a guard came rushing from outside and informed Akbar, "Huzoor, one of your ministers from a bordering town is here and is asking permission to see you".

"Sure, send him in".

The minister came in, bowed down to the king and said, "It is good to see you after some time, but today I have come to see you for a small problem. I could not solve it myself, that is why I am here for its solution".

"Yes, Speak, what is your problem? I will solve whatever I can," the king said.

The Minister called two men and asked them to explain their case themselves to the king. One of them greeted the king and said, "Huzoor, my name is Aameer. I am a trader and I own a lot of lands. This man claims that I am his servant. He also claims that I have stolen his money and disguised myself as him".

The second man stepped forward, greeted the king and said, "Huzoor my name is Aameer, and I am the trader who owns a lot of lands. I went to Afghanistan to do some business for six months, so I left my money and this land under his care and supervision. When I returned from there, I found that he has been using my name to do his business. When I challenged him, he started saying to people that he was Aameer and I was his servant".

Akbar got confused. He did not know who was the real Aameer and who was his servant? He said, "This is a strange case. It is difficult to decide". Then he looked at his courtiers and said, "Is there anyone among you who can solve this case? I will give a bag of gold coins to the one who will solve this case".

As always Birbal smiled and said, "I can solve it, Jahanpanah". He walked to those two men and said to them, "Do you know I can read the mind? You cannot hide the truth from me. Now will you speak the truth yourself or should I tell your minds to all?" They still stood quiet.

Birbal said to them again, "So you won't tell the truth. Lie down on the floor with your face down". Now I will close my eyes, begin to concentrate and will let you know who is speaking the truth and who is telling lie". They did as Birbal said to them. Birbal concentrated for a couple of minutes and then called the guard, "Come here, and cut the head of the servant".

The guard was confused because he did not know who was the servant. As he walked forward, he looked at Birbal helplessly. As the guard came near those people, the first man jumped up and ran to the king's throne and cried, "Forgive me Huzoor. I stole this man's money. I am not Aameer.

❑

23.

Best Flowers

One day, Akbar was taking a walk in his Royal gardens with several courtiers. Many flowers were flowering at that time of the season. A poet pointed out towards a beautiful flower and said, "Look Jahanpanah, how beautiful flower that is? No man can produce such a beautiful thing as this". Birbal was also there. He said, "I don't agree with this, sometimes a man can make more beautiful things than this". Akbar said, "Oh no Birbal, you are talking nonsense. This flower is very beautiful".

After a few days, Birbal presented Akbar with a very skilled craftsman from Agra. He presented a beautiful carved marble bouquet. The emperor was very happy to see it and gave him one thousand gold coins.

Just then a boy came and presented the emperor with a beautiful bouquet of real flowers. "The emperor was very happy to see it too, so he gave a silver coin to the boy. Birbal said, "So the carving was more beautiful than the real thing".

Akbar understood that he had fallen in the hands of his witty minister once again.

❑

24.

The Problem Solver

Several courtiers were vying to be the Royal Advisor of emperor Akbar. So one day, when they came to the court, they said to the emperor, "We want to be your Royal Advisor". Akbar said, "No problem, but you will have to pass the test before you could be my Royal Advisor. And whoever would pass the test will be appointed as my advisor". They agreed.

The king unfastened his waistcloth and lay down on the floor, and asked the candidates to cover him with that cloth from head to toe. Now everybody tried to cover him but in vain. If one wanted to cover the head, then feet remained uncovered or if the feet were covered, then his head remained open.

Just then Birbal entered the court, the king asked Birbal also, if he could cover him with that cloth from head to toe. Birbal paused a moment, then asked the Emperor politely, "Huzoor, Could you pull up your knees a little bit?" The king did so, and Birbal could cover him from head to toe with that cloth.

Realizing that they failed the test, the courtiers left the court quietly and then they never thought about being the King's Advisor.

❑

25.

Why the Camel's neck is Crooked?

As you all know, Emperor Akbar was very impressed with Birbal's wisdom and greatly enjoyed his quick wit. One fine morning when Akbar was especially pleased with Birbal, as a gesture of appreciation, he promised to reward him with many valuable and beautiful gifts.

However, many days passed, and still, there was no sign of even one gift. Birbal was quite disappointed with the king. Then one day, when Akbar was strolling down the banks of the River Yamuna with his ever-faithful Birbal at his side, he happened to notice a camel passing by. He asked Birbal why the neck of the camel was crooked. Birbal thought for a second and promptly replied that it might be because the camel may have forgotten to honour a promise. The holy books mention that those who break their word get punished with a crooked neck; perhaps that was the reason for the camel's crooked neck.

Akbar soon realised his folly of making a promise to Birbal for gifts and not honouring it. He was ashamed of himself. As soon as they returned to the palace he immediately gave Birbal his justly deserved reward. As you can see, Birbal always managed to get what he wanted without directly asking for it.

❑

26.

Foolish Brahmin

Once upon a time, a foolish brahmin came to visit Birbal with a strange request. He wanted to be addressed as 'pandit'. Now, the term 'pandit' refers to a man of learning. But unfortunately, this poor brahmin was uneducated. Birbal tried to explain the difference to him saying that it was not correct to call an uneducated man a pandit and because of this very reason it would be improper to call him so. But the silly brahmin had his heart set on this title.

So, as usual, Birbal had a brilliant idea. He said that as the brahmin was an uneducated man he should hurl abuses and stones at anyone who dared to address him by the very same title he wanted. Then Birbal called all his servants to himself and ordered them to call this lowly brahmin a pandit. The brahmin was very pleased. But the moment the servants started calling out to him as 'pandit' he pretended to be very angry and started to abuse them loudly. Then he picked up a few stones and hurled them in their direction. All as per clever Birbal's advice.

All this shouting and screaming drew a crowd. When people realised that this brahmin was erupting every time anyone called him 'pandit', they all started to tease him. Over the next couple of days, he would constantly hear the refrain 'pandit' wherever he went. Very soon the whole town started referring to him as 'pandit' much to his delight.

The foolish brahmin never realised why people were calling him in this manner. And was extremely pleased with the result. He thanked Birbal from the very bottom of his foolish heart.

❑

27.

Power of Words

One night, Akbar had a dream that he had lost all his teeth except one. Akbar got greatly disturbed by that strange dream.

Next morning, he called his astrologer and asked him about the meaning of his dream.

The astrologer replied, "My Lord, this dream was an indication that all his relatives would die one by one before him".

Akbar became very angry and sad. He asked him to leave his court. Later he asked several other astrologers about the meaning of his dream but all replied same.

Akbar became very sad and was distressed by the interpretation. He sent all astrologers back without giving them anything in return for their interpretation.

A few days later, Akbar met Birbal and told him about his worry. he told him about his dream and interpretation of all the astrologers.

Birbal listened to him and then thought for a while.

Then he said, “My Lord, you don’t need to worry. That dream meant that you will live a longer and more fulfilling life than any of your relatives”.

Akbar cheered up when he heard Birbal’s version and rewarded him handsomely.

Birbal had also conveyed the same thing as the astrologers to the emperor but in an intelligent manner.

❑

28.

Friend's Promise

Once Birbal and his friend were going somewhere. On their way, they had to pass a small stream, on which there was an old bridge which was so narrow that only one person could pass at a time and with time it had become too slippery.

When they reached there, Birbal managed to get across safely but when his friend tried to cross that bridge as soon as he was going to reach another side he lost his balance and fell into the water.

Birbal immediately leaned down and stretched out his hand toward his friend to help him. His friend quickly grasped his hand, then Birbal started to pull his friend towards the shore.

Birbal was tightly holding his friend hand and pulling him toward shore. A friend felt thankful toward Birbal and said, "My friend, thank you for saving my life". And hastily promised him that he would give him a big amount of money in return for saving his life.

Birbal stoically replied, "Thank you..!" And just then let go of his hand and his friend went back into the water with a splash.

His friend was almost on the shore, so with the little struggle, he was finally on the shore where Birbal was standing.

The friend was shocked at his act and questioned, "Why did you do that?"

Birbal smiled and replied, "To take my reward".

The friend said, "But, you could have waited for me to come out of the water safely".

Birbal retorted, "Sure. But couldn't you have waited to come out of the water and stood onshore?"

Birbal's friend realized that he had been hasty in making the promise and was wrong in offering the reward as friends do not help each other for material gains. He apologized to Birbal and thanked him for saving him and driving good sense into him.

❑

29.

God is Everywhere

Once Akbar said to his wise minister Birbal, "You often say that God is everywhere!" So, Akbar took one of his rings out of his finger and said, "Tell me, is your God is in this ring?"

Birbal replied, "Yes, Sure. He certainly is. God is everywhere".

"Can you make me see him?" questioned Akbar.

Birbal asked for sometime to answer that question. Akbar agreed and gave him six months to find an answer and show him, God, in that ring. Birbal went home. Birbal dared not to face Akbar without an answer. So he stayed home thinking about the answer.

One day a little monk came to his home for alms. Seeing Birbal pale face he questioned him the reason for it. Birbal narrated all that transpired between him and the Emperor.

The boy's response was, "Is this what you are worried about? I can give you an answer for this but condition is you have to take me to the emperor and let me meet him personally".

Birbal agreed and the next day took him to court and said, "My lord, Even this little boy can answer that question you asked me!"

Akbar said, "So, little boy show me God in this ring."

The boy replied, "Sure. I will do that but before that can you ask for a glass of curd? I am feeling thirsty".

Akbar orders to bring curd for the boy. The boy took the glass of curd and started to stir it and said, "I am used to drinking good curd which has butter in it but I do not like this stuff which your bearer has brought and which does not yield butter at all".

"Bearer bought the best curd available in this kingdom," replied Akbar.

The boy replied, "Very well, then show me that this curd contains butter in it."

Akbar laughed and replied, "Little boy, you don't know that butter can be got out of curd only after churning it and yet you dare to come here and show me, God!"

"I am not a fool. I just gave you the answer to your question", replied the little boy.

Seeing that Akbar was still puzzled.

The boy said, "Your majesty! In the same manner, God is residing in everything. He is the power that maintains the Universe and yet one cannot see him with one's physical eyes."

❑

30.

Why God takes Human Form?

One day Akbar asked Birbal, "Why does God take human form when he can do everything just by his will?"

After listening to the question, Birbal asked Akbar to give him some time so that he can think of a way to give Akbar a suitable answer to this question.

Akbar agreed to wait.

In the meantime, Birbal went to the room of Akbar's son. There Birbal went to the maid who was looking after Akbar's child and told her, "Today Akbar asked me one philosophical question and I have to give a proper answer to Akbar on that question and for that, I need your help".

Birbal continued, "Now listen carefully. When Akbar come and sit by poolside to play with his child, hide his child inside. Instead, bring a toy-child outside and pretend to tumble near the pool and throw that toy-child into the pool".

In the end, Birbal ensured her that she will not get in trouble for that. She was delighted to help Birbal and agreed to do so.

In the evening as usual routine, Akbar returned from his evening walk and sat on a bench near the pool to play with his son. After sitting there Akbar asked the maid to bring his son there.

As per Birbal's plan while bringing the child to Akbar maid slowly walking by side of pool pretended to lose balance and threw toy-child into the tank.

Akbar at once rushed and jumped into the pool to rescue his son.

Only then Birbal came with Akbar's son and said, "Don't worry. Here is your son".

Akbar got angry at his act and ordered him to be punished for this prank.

Without wasting time Birbal said, "I have given a practical answer to the question you asked me today in the court. Even though there were so many servants to rescue your child still out of affection for your child you jumped into the pool yourself."

❑

31.

Birbal and the Shah

Persia was a country far away from Agra. People who had been to Agra, told the Shah of Persia, many stories about the great Emperor Akbar and his minister, Birbal.

They all praised the witty and clever Birbal and his ever-ready answers.

The Shah of Persia was eager to meet Birbal and test him to see if he was as clever as claimed.

So the Shah sent a man to invite Birbal to Persia.

As Persia was far from Agra, the messenger took many months to reach Akbar's court. On reaching, he conveyed the Shah's invitation to Birbal.

Birbal took permission from Emperor Akbar and set off for Persia along with the messenger.

They reached Persia after a long journey and Birbal was asked to take some rest. The next day he was invited to meet the Shah.

In court, he saw a strange scene.

There were five people dressed in similar clothes, all look like kings. They all sat on the same kind of thrones and they all behaved in the same manner.

The man with Birbal said, "Go and meet the Shah of Persia".

Birbal knew that he had to bow before the Shah and offer his respects but he had never seen the Shah before. How could he recognize the Shah as all the five men were dressed alike?

Birbal looked at the five men sitting on the thrones, from right to left and then left to right, again and again.

Then he went in front of one of them and greeted, "Oh! Great Shah of Persia! Emperor Akbar sends his regards and gifts for you, Your Highness. Have I guessed correctly that out of the five, you are the Shah of Persia?"

"Yes Birbal, you have guessed correctly. I did this to test you. You are clever. I am the real Shah of Persia. Welcome to Persia. But tell me how did you recognize me?" Birbal smiled and said, "Your Majesty.

It was quite simple. When I was looking at you, all these other four men looked at you to see your reaction as the subjects always look up to their king for everything. They looked at you wondering as to what you were thinking. But you were not looking at them. You were looking straight at me. So I knew that you are the real Shah of Persia".

"Birbal, you are very clever," said the Shah of Persia. "I am so glad to meet you. Now I know why everyone always praises you. Well done Birbal".

The Shah of Persia then honoured Birbal with the title, 'Ocean of Intelligence', for being so clever and also presented him many gifts when Birbal returned to Akbar's court.

❑

32.

A Search for Birbal

One day, Emperor Akbar got angry with Birbal over something and told him to leave his court and never come back.

Birbal went home thinking, “The emperor is angry with me. If I stay here or in my country house, he might give me a heavier punishment”.

Birbal decided to hide in an unknown place for some time so that the Emperor would start missing him.

Soon after, Akbar began to miss Birbal because, with the clever Birbal around, he could talk about interesting things.

So he ordered that Birbal should be called back to the court. But Birbal was not to be found anywhere.

Akbar became very worried. He also got quite bored and wanted Birbal to come back to make his life more interesting and livelier.

Akbar thought, "Where can Birbal go? He must be hiding in some far-off village".

So one day, he thought of a plan to get Birbal back. He called all his messengers and told them to go to all the village chiefs around Agra and tell them to reach Agra within fifteen days.

Akbar said, "But tell all the chiefs that on the way to Agra, they have to walk partly in the sun and partly in the shade".

The chiefs found the order strange but none could defy the king's orders.

After a few days, Akbar saw the chiefs walking into the courtyard towards the court. Some of the chiefs had a piece of cloth on their heads. Some were trying to walk half in the sun and a half in the shade formed by pillars.

But one man was carrying a cot, with his hands holding it over his head. It was a cot woven with jute ropes.

So, wherever there were ropes, there was shade and through the gaps, the sun was shining on the man. It was half shade and half sunny under the cot.

Akbar asked his courtiers to bring that man to him.

Akbar said, "Very good, my man. You win. But tell me, who gave you this idea or you will be punished?"

The man said, "My Lord! The man is a friend's friend and has recently come to stay with him".

Akbar knew that Birbal was the only one who could have thought of this.

Akbar said, 'Tell that stranger to come and see me at once. By the way, what is the stranger's name?"

The village chief said, "His name is Birbal but he won't come. He was saying that you are angry with him".

"I have pardoned Birbal and I am no longer angry with him. Tell him that he must come back at once to Agra. I am waiting for him to come back to the court as soon as possible," said Akbar.

When the village chief reached his village, he told Birbal what the emperor had said. Birbal was happy to know that Akbar was no longer angry with him.

When Birbal came back to Agra, Akbar welcomed Birbal and said, “Birbal, see I have got you out of your hiding. This time, I was cleverer than you”.

❑

33.

A Mother's Beautiful Child

Akbar once said to his courtiers, "I think that my grandson, Khurram is a beautiful child. What do you all think?"

The courtiers wanted to please Akbar, so they all said, "Your Highness, Prince Khurram is the most beautiful child".

Birbal kept sitting quietly.

Akbar asked him, "What is the matter Birbal? You don't seem to agree with me and the others in the court. Don't you find my Khurram to be the most beautiful child?"

Birbal stood up and bowed before Akbar and said, "I think it is very difficult to test what is beautiful and what is not. There is no real test for beauty".

Akbar felt bad and said, "No Birbal, I do not agree with you. A rose is beautiful and a crow is ugly to all".

Wanting to prove Birbal wrong, Akbar then said to all the courtiers, "I order each of you to bring a child each, to find the most beautiful child of all".

The next day, all the courtiers, except Birbal, brought a child each.

After looking at all the children, Akbar said, "I still think that my grandson, Khurram is the best looking".

Akbar asked Birbal, "Why have you not brought a child, Birbal?"

"I could not find any child who was perfect," said Birbal.

Akbar asked, "Birbal, you still don't agree that my Khurram is the most handsome out of all the children?"

"Please give me some time. I will have to search for one," said Birbal.

"As you wish, Birbal," Akbar replied.

The next day, Birbal said, "Your Majesty, I have at last found the most beautiful child in Agra, but the mother will not let the child come here because she loves the child a lot".

Akbar said, "We will go to her house and see the child there".

Akbar ordered the courtiers to accompany him to see the child. Everyone quickly got ready to leave, for they all were eager to see the most beautiful child as Birbal had claimed. Then they started walking with Birbal leading the way.

They soon reached the slums where the poor people lived.

Then Birbal stopped and said, "This is where the child lives. We will wait here for some time".

In a short while, a child crawled out from a hut. The courtiers looked at Birbal with surprise because the child was not beautiful at all. Rather the child was the ugliest of all the children the courtiers had brought, and this made Akbar angry.

Akbar shouted, "Birbal! What kind of a joke is this? The child is ugly".

Birbal replied patiently, “Just wait a while, please”.

They kept standing for some time watching the child playing. Suddenly, the child fell and started crying.

A woman came running out of the hut and said, “Oh my dear child, my poor darling, are you hurt?”

The child continued crying and the woman spoke to the child, “Hush, my beautiful child. Don’t cry. You are the apple of my eye. No one is as lovely as you are. I love you more than anything else”.

A courtier exclaimed, “Oh Lord! How can she call this ugly child beautiful?”

The mother of the child heard this and she shouted, “Are you speaking about my child?”

The courtier replied “We are speaking the truth. Your child is ugly”.

The mother screamed, “How dare you talk about my child like this?”

“Go and search for the whole world and you will not find a child more beautiful than mine. Go away from here and dare not speak like that about my child”.

Akbar indicated his courtiers to leave, He turned to Birbal and said, “You have proved your point,

Birbal. You have proved that everyone thinks that their child is the most beautiful".

Birbal smiled and said, "Not only child, Your Majesty, even grandchild!"

Akbar started laughing and said, "Birbal you are right. I find Khurram to be the most beautiful for he is my own. Every parent finds his child to be the most beautiful".

❑

34.

The Root of the Problem

People trusted Birbal, so they often came to him with their problems. One day, a man came running up to Birbal and fell at his feet saying, "Sir, someone has stolen all my money".

Birbal saw how upset the poor man was but he asked, "You are wearing dirty clothes. You look poor, then how can you have money?"

The man said, "Sir, I work very hard in the gardens of the emperor so that I can save money for my old age, as I have no one to look after me. I had saved a thousand gold coins but someone has stolen them. I am ruined".

"First. Tell me where the money was kept", asked Birbal.

"As I work in the gardens of the king, I dug a hole under a pear tree and kept all my money there. But all of it is gone," said the gardener and he started crying.

"Crying will not help you. Stop crying and let me think", said Birbal.

Birbal thought, "The money was in the hole under a pear tree. Who would dig up over there?"

Suddenly, things were clear in Birbal's mind and he said to the gardener, "Go home. I will soon get your money back. But be careful next time and don't keep the money in such an unsafe place. I won't help you if you act so carelessly again".

Birbal summoned all the doctors of the city and asked them about the benefits of the pear tree. He finally asked them, "Does the pear tree help in making any medicines?"

They said, "No".

But one doctor replied, "The fruits and leaves do not help us but the roots have medicinal value".

Birbal asked, "Have you used the roots of the pear tree for any medicine?"

The doctor replied, "Yes, My. Lord. Just a few days back, I made a medicine from the roots of the pear tree. It cured a patient of mine who was very ill".

"Who was that man whom you cured? Go and fetch him," ordered Birbal.

The man came and Birbal asked, "Has this doctor been treating you?"

"Yes Sir, and I am well because of the wonderful medicine he made from the roots of the pear tree, "said the man.

"From where did you get the roots for the medicine?" asked Birbal.

"I sent my servant to get it, Sir, "said the man. So Birbal ordered him to get the servant. The man left at once and came back with the servant.

Birbal asked, "So you helped to cure your master?"

"Yes, Sir. l brought the roots of the pear tree for the medicine, "said the servant.

"Where was the tree?" asked Birbal.

"In the king's garden," said the man.

"Give me a thousand coins at once that you found while digging for the roots under the pear tree," said Birbal.

The scared servant said, “Yes Sir, I will give it back. I have stolen the bag of gold coins and that was a wrong thing to do. Please pardon me”.

“Go get the money, then you will not be punished. You had stolen the money and that was wrong. Since you have confessed, I forgive you”.

The servant ran to get the money and soon gave the bag of thousand gold coins to Birbal.

Then Birbal gave five gold coins to the servant and said, “You can keep these coins for speaking the truth”.

The servant fell at Birbal’s feet and said, “Thank you so much, My Lord. I promise never to steal again”.

Birbal then said to the gardener, “Take your money. I have taken out five gold coins because you were stupid enough to keep your money in an unsafe place. Be careful in the future”.

❑

35.

Birbal, the Child

Birbal arrived late for a function and the emperor was displeased.

"My child was crying and I had to placate him," explained the courtier.

"Does it take so long to calm down a child?" asked the emperor. "It appears you know nothing about child-rearing. Now you pretend to be a child and I shall act as your father and I will show you how you should have dealt with your child. Go on. Ask me for whatever he asked of you".

"I want a cow," said Birbal.

Akbar ordered a cow to be brought to the palace.

"I want its milk. I want its milk," said Birbal, imitating the voice of a small child.

"Milk the cow and give to him," said Akbar to his servants.

The cow was milked and the milk was offered to Birbal. He drank a little and then handed the bowl back to Akbar.

"Now put the rest of it back into the cow, put it back, put in back, put it back", wailed Birbal.

The emperor was flabbergasted and quietly left the room.

❑

36

The Servant

One day, Akbar and Birbal were riding through the countryside and they happened to pass by a cabbage patch.

"Cabbages are such delightful vegetables!" said Akbar. "I just love cabbage".

"The cabbage is the king of vegetables!" said Birbal.

A few weeks later they were riding past the cabbage patch again.

This time, however, the emperor made a face when he saw the vegetables. "I used to love cabbage but now I have no taste for it," said Akbar.

"The cabbage is a tasteless vegetable", agreed Birbal.

The emperor was astonished.

"But the last time you said it was the king of vegetables!" he said.

"I did," admitted Birbal. "But I am your servant Your Majesty, not the cabbage's".

❑

37.

Wise One

Ram and Sham both claimed ownership of the same mango tree.

One day they approached Birbal and asked him to settle the dispute.

Birbal said to them, "There is only one way to settle the matter. Pluck all the fruits on the tree and divide them equally between the two of you. Then cut down the tree and divide the wood".

Ram thought it was a fair judgment and said so.

But Sham was horrified.

"Your Honour," he said to Birbal. "I've tended that tree for seven years. I'd rather let Ram have it than see it cut down".

"Your concern for the tree has told me all I wanted to know," said Birbal, and declared Sham the true owner of the tree.

❑

38.

Cooking the Khichdi

It was winter. The ponds were all frozen.

At the court, Akbar asked Birbal, "Tell me Birbal! Will, a man do anything for money?" Birbal replied, "Yes".

The emperor ordered him to prove it.

The next day, Birbal came to the court along with a poor Brahmin who merely had a penny left with him. His family was starving.

Birbal told the king that the Brahmin was ready to do anything for the sake of money.

The king ordered the Brahmin to be inside the frozen pond throughout the night without any attire if he needs the money.

The poor Brahmin had no choice. The whole night, he was inside the pond shivering. He returned to the durbar the next day to receive his reward.

The king asked, "Tell me, Oh poor Brahmin! How could you withstand the extreme temperature all through the night?"

The innocent Brahmin replied, "I could see a faintly glowing light a kilometre away and I withstood with that ray of light".

Akbar refused to pay the Brahmin his reward saying that he had got warmth from the light and withstood the cold and that was cheating.

The poor Brahmin could not argue with him and so he returned disappointed and bare-handed.

Birbal tried to explain to the king but the king was in no mood to listen to him.

Thereafter, Birbal stopped coming to the durbar and sent a messenger to the king saying that he would come to the court only after cooking his khichdi.

As Birbal did not turn up even after 5 days, the king himself went to Birbal's house to see what he was doing. Birbal had lit the fire and kept the pot of uncooked khichdi one meter away from it.

Akbar questioned him, “How will the khichdi get cooked with the fire one meter away? What is wrong with you Birbal?”

Birbal, cooking the khichdi, replied, “Oh my great King of Hindustan! When it was possible for a person to receive warmth from a light that was a kilometre away, then it is possible for this khichdi, which is just a meter away from the source of heat, to get cooked”.

Akbar understood his mistake. He called the poor Brahmin and rewarded him 2000 gold coins.

❑

39.

Half the Reward

Mahesh Das was a citizen in the kingdom of Akbar. He was an intelligent young man.

Once when Akbar went hunting in the jungle, he lost his way. Mahesh Das who lived in the outskirts helped the king reach the palace. The emperor rewarded him with his ring.

The emperor also promised to give him a responsible posting at his court. After a few days, Mahesh Das went to the court. The guard did not allow him to enter.

Mahesh Das showed the ring to the guard which the king had given him. Now the guard thought that the young man was sure to get more rewards by the king. The greedy guard agreed to allow him inside the court on one condition. It was that, Mahesh Das had to pay him half the reward he would get from the emperor. Mahesh Das accepted the condition.

He then entered the court and showed the ring to the king.

The king who recognized Mahesh asked him, "Oh young man! What do you expect as a reward from the King of Hindustan?" "Majesty! I expect 50 lashes from you as a reward," replied Mahesh Das. The courtiers were stunned. They thought that he was mad. Akbar pondered over his request and asked him the reason.

Mahesh Das said he would tell him the reason after receiving his reward. Then the king's men whipped him as per his wish. After the 25th lash, Mahesh Das requested the King to call the guard who was at the gate.

The guard appeared before the king. He was happy at the thought that he was called to be rewarded. But to his surprise, Mahesh Das told the King, "Jahanpanah! This greedy guard let me inside on condition that I pay him half the reward I receive from you. I wanted to teach him a lesson. Please give the remaining 25 lashes to this guard so that I can keep my promise to him".

The king then ordered that the guard be given 25 lashes along with 5 years of imprisonment. The king was very happy with Mahesh Das. He called him 'RAJA BIRBAL' and made him his chief minister.

❑

40.

Identify the Guest

Birbal had been invited to lunch by a rich man.

Birbal went to the man's house and found him in a hall full of people. His host greeted him warmly.

"I did not know there would be so many guests," said Birbal who hated large gatherings.

"They are not guests," said the man. "They are my employees, all except one man. He is the only other guest here beside you".

Then a crafty look came on the man's face.

"Can you tell me which of them is the guest?" he asked.

"Maybe I could," said Birbal. "Talk to them as I observe them. Tell them a joke or something".

The man told a joke that Birbal thought was perhaps the worst he had heard in a long time. When he finished everyone laughed uproariously.

"Well," said the rich man. "I've told my joke. Now tell me who my other guest is".

Birbal pointed out the man to him.

"How did you know?" asked his host, amazed.

"Employees tend to laugh at any joke told by their employers," explained Birbal. "When I saw that this man was the only one not laughing at your joke and looked positively bored, I at once knew he was your other guest".

❑

41.

Just One Question

One Day, a scholar came to the court of the emperor Akbar and challenged Birbal to answer his questions and thus prove that he was as clever as people said he was.

He asked Birbal, "Would you prefer to answer a hundred easy questions or just a single difficult one?"

Both the emperor and Birbal had had a difficult day and were impatient to leave.

"Ask me one difficult question," said Birbal.

"Well, then, tell me," said the man. "Which came first into the world, the chicken or the egg?"

"The chicken," replied Birbal.

"How do you know?" asked the scholar, a note of triumph in his voice.

"We had agreed you would ask only one question and you have already asked it," said Birbal and he and the emperor walked away leaving the scholar gaping.

❑

42.

The Noble Beggar

Emperor Akbar asked Birbal if a man could be the lowest and the noblest at the same time.

"It is possible," said Birbal.

"Then bring me such a person," said the emperor.

Birbal went out and returned with a beggar.

"He is the lowest among your subjects," he said, presenting him to Akbar.

"That might be true," said Akbar. "But I don't see how he can be the noblest".

"He has been given the honour of an audience with the emperor," said Birbal. "That makes him the noblest among beggars".

❑

43.

Painting by Birbal

Once Akbar told Birbal, “Birbal, make me a painting. Use your imagination in it”.

To which the reply was, “But Huzoor, I am a minister, how can I possibly paint?”

The king was angry and said, “If I don’t get a good painting by one week then you shall be hanged!”

The clever Birbal had an idea.

After one week, he went to the court and with him, he carried a covered frame.

Akbar was happy to see that Birbal had obeyed him until he opened the cover. The courtiers rushed to see what was wrong. What they saw made them feel very happy.

At last, they would not see Birbal in court! The painting was of nothing but of the ground and sky. There were a few specs of green on the ground.

The emperor angrily asked Birbal, "What is this?" To which the reply was, "A cow eating grass Huzoor!"

Akbar asked, "Where are the cow and grass?" Birbal replied, "I used my imagination Huzoor. The cow ate the grass and returned to its shed!"

❑

44.

Question for Question

One day Akbar said to Birbal, "Can you tell me how many bangles your wife wears?"

Birbal said he could not.

"You cannot?" exclaimed Akbar. "You see her hands every day while she serves you food. Yet you do not know how many bangles she has on her hands? How is that?"

"Let us go down to the garden, Your Majesty", said Birbal. "And I'll tell you".

They went down the small staircase that led to the garden. Then Birbal turned to the emperor, "Your Majesty," he said, "You go up and down this staircase every day. Can you tell me how many steps there are in the staircase?"

The emperor grinned sheepishly and quickly changed the subject.

❑

45.

The Blind Saint

There lived a blind saint in an ashram in the kingdom of Emperor Akbar.

He was believed to prophesised the future correctly.

Once he had visitors who had come to treat their niece. The child's parents were killed in front of the girl's eyes. Once she saw the saint, she started to scream saying that that saint was the culprit.

Angered by the girl's words, the saint demanded the couple to get away with their child.

The whole day the girl cried which made the couple to realize that the girl was not lying.

Therefore, they decided to seek the help of Birbal.

Birbal consoled them and asked them to wait at the emperor's assembly. Birbal had invited the saint to Akbar's court too.

Then in front of all the ministers, he drew a sword and neared the saint to kill him. The saint in bewilderment immediately drew another sword and began to fight. Thus, by this act of the saint, it was proved that he wasn't blind.

Therefore, Akbar demanded to hang the culprit and rewarded the girl for her bravery for telling the truth even at the critical situation.

❑

46.

The Jealous Courtiers

One day, emperor Akbar was inspecting the law and order situation in the kingdom. One of his ministers, who was jealous of Raja Birbal, complained that the emperor gave importance only to Birbal's suggestions and all the other ministers were ignored.

Akbar wanted the minister to know how wise Birbal was.

There was a marriage procession going on.

The emperor ordered the minister to enquire whose marriage it was. The minister found out and walked towards the emperor wearing a proud expression on his face.

Then the king called Birbal and asked him too to enquire whose marriage was going on. When Birbal returned, Akbar asked the minister, “Where are the couple going?” The minister said that the king had only asked him to enquire whose marriage was going on.

Then Akbar asked Birbal the same question. “O My Majesty! They are going to the city of Allahabad,” replied Raja Birbal. Now the King turned towards the minister and said, “Now do you understand why Birbal is more important to me? It is not enough if you complete a task. You have to use your intelligence to do a little more work”. The minister’s face fell. He had learnt the importance of Birbal, the hard way.

❑

47.

The Loyal Gardener

One day, Emperor Akbar stumbled on a rock in his garden. He was in a foul mood that day and the accident made him so angry that he ordered the gardener's arrest and execution.

The next day, when the gardener was asked what his last wish was before he was hanged, he requested an audience with the emperor.

This wish was granted, but when the man neared the throne, he loudly cleared his throat and spat at the emperor's feet.

The emperor was taken aback and demanded to know why he had done such a thing. The gardener had acted on Birbal's advice and now Birbal stepped forward in the man's defence.

"Your Majesty," he said. "There could be no person more loyal to you than this unfortunate man. Fearing that people would say you hanged him for a trifle, he has gone out of his way to give you a genuine reason for hanging him".

The emperor, realizing that he had been about to do great injustice, set the man free.

❑

48.

The Musical Genius

Famous musicians once gathered at Akbar's court for a competition.

The one who could capture a bull's interest was to be declared the winner.

One by one, they played the most heavenly music but the bull paid no attention.

Then Birbal took the stage. His music sounded like the droning of mosquitoes and the mooing of cows.

But to everyone's amazement, the bull suddenly became alert and began to move in a lively manner.

Akbar declared Birbal the winner.

❑

49.

The Sadhu

Akbar came to the throne when he was only thirteen years old. In the years that followed, he built one of the greatest empires of his time. He lived in unimaginable splendour. He was surrounded by courtiers who agreed with every word he said, who flattered him and treated him as if he were a God. Perhaps it was not surprising that Emperor Akbar was sometimes arrogant and behaved as if the whole world belonged to him.

One day, Birbal decided to make the great emperor stop and think about life.

That evening as the emperor was going towards his palace, he noticed a Sadhu lying in the centre of his garden. He could not believe his eyes. A strange Sadhu, in ragged clothes, right in the middle of the palace garden? The guards would have to be punished for this, though the emperor is furious as he walked over to that Sadhu and prodded him with the tip of his embroidered slipper.

"Here, fellow!" he cried. "What are you doing here? Get up and go away at once!"

The Sadhu opened his eyes. Then he sat up slowly. "Huzoor," he said in a sleepy voice. "Is this your garden, then?"

"Yes!" cried the Emperor. "This garden, those rose bushes, the fountain beyond that, the courtyard, the palace, this fort, this empire, it all belongs to me!"

Slowly that Sadhu stood up. "And the river, Huzoor? And the city? And this country?"

"Yes, yes, it's all mine", said the emperor. "Now get out!"

"Ah", said the Sadhu. "And before you, Huzoor. Who did the garden, fort and city belong to then?"

"My father, of course", said the emperor. Despite his irritation, he was beginning to get interested in the Sadhu's questions. He loved philosophical discussions and he could tell, from his manner of speaking, that the Sadhu was a learned man.

"And who was here before him?" the Sadhu asked quietly.

"His father, my father's father, as you know".

"Ah", said the Sadhu. "So this garden, those rose bushes, the palace and the fort all this has only belonged to you for your lifetime. Before that they belonged to your father, am I right? And after your time they will belong to your son, and then to his son?"

"Yes", said Emperor Akbar wonderingly.

"So each one stays here for a time and then goes on his ways?"

"Yes".

"Like a Dharamshala?" the Sadhu asked. "No one owns a Dharamshala. Or the shade of a tree on the side of a road. We stop and rest for a while and then goes on. And someone has always been there before us and someone will always come after we have gone. Is that not so?"

"It is", Emperor Akbar quietly.

"So your garden, your palace, your fort, your empire... these are only places you will stay in for a time, for the span of your lifetime. When you die, they will no longer belong to you. You will go, leaving them in the possession of someone else, just as your father did and his father before him".

Emperor Akbar nodded. "The whole world is a Dharamshala", he said slowly, thinking very hard. "In which we mortals rest awhile. That's what you are telling me, isn't it? Nothing on this earth can ever belong to a single person, because each person is only passing through the earth and must die one day?"

The Sadhu nodded solemnly. Then, bowing to the ground, he removed his white beard and saffron turban and his voice changed. "Jahanpanah, forgive me!" he said, in his normal voice. "It was my way of asking you to think about."

"Birbal, oh, Birbal!" the emperor exclaimed. "You are wiser than any philosopher. Come, come at once to the royal chamber and let us discuss this further. Even emperors are but wayfarers on the path of life, it is clear!"

❑

50.

The Sharpest Spears and Shields

A man who made spears and shields once came to Akbar's court.

"Your Majesty, nobody can make shields and spears equal to mine," he said. "My shields are so strong that nothing can pierce them and my spears are so sharp that there's nothing they cannot pierce".

"I can certainly prove you wrong on one count," said Birbal suddenly.

"Impossible!" declared the man.

"Hold up one of your shields and I will pierce it with one of your spears," said Birbal with a smile.

❑

51.

The Well Dispute

Once there was a complaint at King Akbar's court.

Two neighbours shared their garden. In that garden, there was a well that was possessed by Iqbal Khan. His neighbour, who was a farmer wanted to buy the well for irrigation purpose. Therefore, they signed an agreement between them, after which the farmer-owned the well.

Even after selling the well to the farmer, Iqbal continued to fetch water from the well. Angered by this, the farmer had come to get justice from King Akbar.

King Akbar asked Iqbal the reason for fetching water from the well even after selling it to the farmer.

Iqbal replied that he had sold only the well to the farmer but not the water inside it.

King Akbar wanted Birbal, who was present in the court listening to the problem, to solve the dispute.

Birbal came forward and gave a solution. He said, "Iqbal, You say that you have sold only the well to the farmer. And you claim that the water is yours. Then how come you can keep your water inside another person's well without paying rent?"

Iqbal's trickery was countered thus in a tricky way. The farmer got justice and Birbal was fairly rewarded.

❑

52.

What the Drop Taketh!

The anecdotes of Emperor Akbar and his trusted aide Birbal are entertaining as well as enlightening. Once, the emperor received the gift of a rare perfume. As he opened the bottle, a drop of perfume fell to the floor. Akbar instinctively moved to retrieve it by wiping the floor with his finger. As he looked up he noticed a bemused look on Birbal's face, his eyes seemed to mock the emperor for being scrounging.

To change Birbal's perception, Akbar summoned him the next morning to his bath. He asked his attendants to fill up the bathtub with the best of perfumes. Akbar sought to show Birbal that as emperor he could afford to waste as much perfume as he wanted. Birbal when asked to react said the immortal lines, “An entire tub full cannot retrieve what the drop took away!”

Birbal sought to tell the emperor that his earlier instinctive action (that exhibited miserliness) could not be undone by an intentional action (aimed at big-heartedness). Our character is determined by our reactions, not by forced posturing. It is better to be transparent then wear favourable masks. Every little action and reaction, every spoken word and emerging thought reflects our true self!

❑

53.

The Pot of the Wit

Once Emperor Akbar became very angry at his favourite minister Birbal. He asked Birbal to leave the kingdom and go away. Accepting the command of the emperor, Birbal left the kingdom and started working in a farmer's farm in an unknown village far away under a different identity.

As months passed, Akbar started to miss Birbal. He was struggling to solve many issues in the empire without Birbal's advice. He regretted his decision of asking Birbal to leave the empire in anger. So Akbar sent his soldiers to find Birbal, but they failed to find him. No one knew where Birbal was. Akbar finally found a trick. He sent a message to the head of every village to send a pot full of the wit to the emperor. If the pot full of wit cannot be sent, fill the pot with diamonds and jewels.

This message also reached Birbal, who lived in one of the villages. The people of the village got together. All started talking about what to do now? Wit is not a thing, which can be filled in the pot. How will we arrange for diamonds and jewels to fill the pot and send to the emperor? Birbal who was sitting among the villagers said, "Give me the pot, I will fill the wit in one month's end". Everyone trusted Birbal and agreed to give him a chance. They still didn't know his identity.

Birbal took the pot with him and went back to the farm. He had planted watermelons on his farm. He selected a small watermelon and without cutting it from the plant, he put that in the pot. He started looking after it by providing water and fertilizer regularly. Within a few days, the watermelon grew into a pot so much that it was impossible to get it out of the pot.

Soon, the watermelon reached to the same size as the pot from inside. Birbal then cut the watermelon from the vine and separated it with the pot. Later, he sent a pot to Emperor Akbar with a message that "Please remove the wit without cutting it from the pot and without breaking the pot".

Akbar watched the watermelon in the pot and realized that this can only be Birbal's Work. Akbar himself came to the village, took Birbal back with him.

❑

54.

Wicked Barber's Plight

As we all know, Birbal was not only Emperor Akbar's favourite minister but also a minister dearly loved by most of the commoners, because of his ready wit and wisdom. People used to come to him from far and wide for advice on personal matters too. However, there was a group of ministers that were jealous of his growing popularity and disliked him intensely. They outwardly showered him with praise and compliments, but on the inside, they began to hatch a plot to kill him.

One day they approached the king's barber with a plan. As the barber was extremely close to the king, they asked him to help them get rid of Birbal permanently. And of course, they promised him a huge sum of money in return. The wicked barber readily agreed.

The next time the king required his services, the barber started a conversation about the emperor's father who he also used to serve. He sang praises of his fine, and silky-smooth hair. And then as an afterthought, he asked the king that as he was enjoying such great prosperity, had he attempted to do anything for the welfare of his ancestors?

The king was furious at such impertinent stupidity and told the barber that it was not possible to do anything because they were already dead. The barber mentioned that he knew of a magician who could come of help. The magician could send a person up to heaven to enquire about his father's welfare. But of course, this person would have to be chosen carefully; he would have to be intelligent enough to follow the magician's instructions as well as make on-the-spot decisions. He must be wise, intelligent and responsible. The barber then suggested the best person for the job – the wisest of all ministers, Birbal.

The king was very excited about hearing from his dead father and asked the barber to go ahead and make the arrangements immediately. He asked him what was needed to be done. The barber explained that they would take Birbal in a procession to the burial grounds and light a pyre. The magician would then chant some 'mantras' as Birbal would ascend to the heavens through the smoke. The chanting would help protect Birbal from the fire.

The king happily informed Birbal of this plan. Birbal said that he thought it a brilliant idea and wanted to know the brain behind it. When learning that it was the barber's idea, he agreed to go to heaven on condition that he be given a large sum of money for the long journey as well as one month to settle his family so that they had no trouble while he was gone. The king agreed to both conditions.

In this month, he got a few trustworthy men to build a tunnel from the funeral grounds to his house. And on the day of the ascension, after the pyre had been lit, Birbal escaped through the concealed door of the tunnel. He disappeared into his house where he hid for a few months while his hair and beard grew long and unruly.

In the meantime, his enemies were rejoicing as they thought that they had seen the last of Birbal. Then one day after many, many months Birbal arrived at the palace with news of the king's father. The king was extremely pleased to see him and ready with a barrage of questions. Birbal told the king that his father was in the best of spirits and had been provided with all the comforts except one.

The king wanted to know what was lacking because now he thought he had found a way to send things and people to heaven. Birbal answered that there were no barbers in heaven, which is why even he was forced to grow his beard. He said that his father had asked for a good barber.

So the king decided to send his barber to serve his father in heaven. He called both the barber and the magician to prepare to send him to heaven. The barber could say absolutely nothing in his defence as he was caught in his trap. And once the pyre was lit, he died on the spot.

Nobody dared to conspire against Birbal again.

❑

55.

Birbal's Wisdom

One fine day, Akbar lost his ring. When Birbal arrived in the court, Akbar told him, "I have lost my ring. My father had given it to me as a gift. Please help me find it". Birbal said, "Do not worry Your Majesty, I will find your ring right now."

He said, "Your Majesty the ring is here in this court itself, it is with one of the courtiers. The courtier who has a straw in his beard has your ring". The courtier who had the emperor's ring was shocked and immediately moved his hand over his beard. Birbal noticed this act of the courtier. He immediately pointed towards the courtier and said, "Please search this man. He has the emperor's ring".

Akbar could not understand how Birbal had managed to find the ring. Birbal then told Akbar that a guilty person is always scared.

❑

56.

The Number of Crows

Akbar and Birbal were taking a stroll in the king's garden one pleasant morning. Akbar saw the crows in his garden and wondered how many crows there are in his kingdom. He posed the question to Birbal.

How many crows can you find in Akbar's kingdom?

Birbal gave it some thought and said that there are ninety thousand, two hundred and forty-nine crows in the kingdom. Akbar was amazed by his quick response and asked him, "What if there is a higher number of crows than the number you just mentioned?". Birbal replied, "Then, crows from the neighbouring kingdoms must be visiting". Then Akbar asked, "What if the number is fewer than what you mentioned?". Birbal calmly replied, "Then, the crows must have gone on a vacation to the neighbouring kingdom".

❑

57.

The Foolish Thief

Once upon a time, a rich merchant was robbed in King Akbar's kingdom. The grief-stricken merchant went to the court and asked for help. Akbar asked Birbal to help the merchant find the robber. The merchant told Birbal that he was suspicious of one of his servants. On getting the hint from the merchant, Birbal summoned all the servants and told them to stand in a straight line.

When asked about the robbery, everyone denied doing it, as expected. Birbal then handed over one stick of the same length, to each one of them. While dispersing, Birbal said, "By tomorrow, the robber's stick will increase by two inches".

The next day when Birbal summoned everyone and inspected their sticks, one servant's stick was shorter by two inches. On being asked by the merchant about the mystery of finding the real thief, Birbal said, "It was simple: the thief had cut his stick by two inches, fearing that it would increase in size".

❑

58.

Licking Each Other

Akbar and Birbal were in the habit of teasing one another. They never missed a chance. And, if they did not get a chance, they created one. That was a day when there was no chance to tease. Akbar was disappointed. He thought his day would be incomplete without teasing Birbal. So he started to spin a story.

Akbar started to laugh aloud suddenly. His courtiers were astonished. "Your Highness, may we know what makes you laugh so suddenly?"

they asked in chorus. "I will tell you," said Akbar and he continued, "Yesterday I had a funny dream. Birbal and I were having a stroll on the banks of the Yamuna.

Suddenly we were swept away by the river in different directions. After some time, we drifted into two corners, Birbal in one and myself in the other. There lies the joke.

I was washed by sweet water scented by perfumes. I raised my eyes to see Birbal lying in a swamp filled with dirt and gutter. He was soaked in filth and foul smell".

The courtiers also joined in the joke and laughed. Birbal humbly stood and said, "What a coincidence Your Highness!". "What are you telling Birbal?" asked Akbar.

"Your Highness, the only difference in our dreams is that my dream did not end there. After getting out from the corners we started cleaning one another.

I had to lick you clean and you know what you did! You started licking me clean despite my refusal". Akbar had to spare Birbal because it was he, who started the row.

❑

59.

Truth and False

Birbal's witty answers always pleased Emperor Akbar. Hence, Birbal was often asked difficult and tricky questions by the emperor. One day, when both of them were going hunting, Akbar came up with a question. He asked, "Can you tell me what is the difference between true and false?"

Birbal could not come up with an answer immediately. He remained thoughtful for a few minutes. Akbar felt proud that he had finally asked a question that Birbal found difficult.

The Emperor asked with a grin, "Is the question too difficult for you?" Birbal soon answered confidently, "Your majesty, the difference between true and false is the distance between the eyes and the ears".

This was a strange answer and it confused the emperor. Akbar questioned, "How is my question related to eyes and ears? Explain yourself". "Your Majesty, what you see with your eyes is always true. What you hear with your ears is generally false".

The emperor was pleased and satisfied with the answer. On returning to the palace, Birbal was showered with costly gifts.

❑

60.

The Strange Question

One of Emperor Akbar's favourite pastime was to test the wit of his ministers. One fine day, in the court, Akbar announced, "There is a question I want to ask all my courtiers. I will reward the one, who answers it correctly". The courtiers became very excited and encouraged the king, "What is the question, Your Majesty?"

The king smiled and asked, "Is there anything that cannot be seen by the sun or the moon?" The courtiers were puzzled. They thought deeply but it was of no use. Time went by and soon it was late in the evening. Yet, none of the courtiers could come up with a satisfying answer.

It had become time for the ministers to go home. Akbar was giving the last speech for the day. He said, "I feel upset that none of you could come up with an answer! Hmm... I was planning to give this jewellery set as a reward. It has rare gems in it. Alas! No one is worthy enough to wear it".

It was then, that Birbal stood up and said, "Your majesty, I have the answer to your question, darkness is something that cannot be seen by the sun or the moon". "Excellent! That's exactly the answer I was searching for," exclaimed the happy emperor. The emperor called Birbal and gave him the jewellery set. The courtiers looked on in jealousy.

❑

61.

Big and Small Line

The scholars in the palace had gathered for a discussion. They were seated in a circle. Each one was boasting about one's wisdom. Akbar happened to be passing by, he overheard the discussion and came towards them. When the scholars saw the emperor, they immediately stood up in respect. "I know each one of you is clever. I would, however, like to find out who among you is the cleverest," said the emperor. This excited the scholars. "Certainly, Your Majesty, if that's your wish," they said. Akbar used the dipstick of slaked lime to draw a line on the marble floor in front of them. He then declared, "The one who can make this line smaller will be rewarded." "That's so easy," thought the scholars.

The emperor continued, "There is one condition. No one is allowed to make any changes to the line that is drawn". The scholars were at a loss. "How is that possible? To make a line smaller, it would be required to rub off a small portion of it". They kept on thinking of some other way but could find none.

Birbal waited to see if anyone could come up with an answer. When no one stepped forward, he spoke up, "Please, give me that dipstick, Your Majesty. "He took it from the emperor and drew a bigger line next to the earlier one. The emperor burst out laughing and said, "You have proved you are the cleverest. Hahaha, here is a reward for you". The emperor rewarded Birbal, while the scholars hung their heads in shame.

❑

62.

The Use of Weapons and Wits

Once Akbar and Birbal were taking a walk when Akbar asked Birbal, "Birbal, In the face of danger from an enemy, what will you use? Your wits or some weapon?" Birbal replied, "One's wit will always help him through any problem. So instead of a weapon, I will rely on my wits first."

Akbar argued that any weapon is the best thing to be used when in danger of an attack. They continued to argue on this point.

Meanwhile, a mad elephant got loose and suddenly came in front of them. Akbar immediately removed his sword and started to fight with the elephant, but the sword was too small for the elephant and he soon broke it. Birbal saw a wall. He and the emperor quickly climbed the wall to escape from the mad elephant.

Birbal said, “See Your Majesty! Your sword was not able to protect us, but with just our wits we were able to save ourselves by climbing on to the wall”. Akbar agreed and happily accepted Birbal’s theory that wits are more important than any weapon.

❑

63.

The Green Horse

One day, Akbar was riding a horse in a garden. Birbal was also with him. There was greenery all around. Akbar was happy to see the surroundings. He said to himself, "What a pleasure it will be to ride a green horse in a garden like this".

Immediately, Akbar ordered Birbal, "You must get me a green horse within seven days. If you fail to get it, then don't show me your face ever again!" "A green horse? There can't be a green horse," Birbal thought to himself. Both of them knew this but Akbar just wanted to test Birbal's wisdom.

Birbal spent seven days looking for such a horse. On the eighth day, Birbal presented himself before Akbar. He said, "Your Highness, I have found a green horse". Akbar was surprised and he asked, "Where is that horse? You must present it to me right away!"

To this, Birbal said, "Your Highness, it is difficult to bring it here. The owner of that horse has put two conditions". Akbar asked, "What are those two conditions?" "Your Highness, according to the first condition, you have to go to get the horse". Akbar agreed and said, "Oh, that's very simple! I will go there to get the horse. What's the second condition?"

"Since the horse is so special, you will have to go to bring it on a special day. The owner insists that you must bring it on the day other than the seven days of the week," Birbal said. He continued, "Your Highness, if you desire to have a green horse, you will have to fulfil these two conditions!"

Akbar was pleased. He was happy with Birbal's wisdom. Akbar realised that it was not possible to fool Birbal.

❑

64.

The Lion's Cage

The emperor of Persia used to send riddles to Akbar. Akbar in return also used to send puzzles to the Persian Emperor. Both were good friends.

Once, the Persian Emperor send a big cage with an artificial lion in it. The lion in the cage looked as though it was real. When the cage arrived in the court, many courtiers were frightened. Some even went to hide behind pillars. Even Emperor Akbar missed a few heartbeats. The lion's mouth was open with two big protruding teeth.

The men who brought the cage saluted the Emperor and said, "Our emperor has sent this cage and he wanted to know whether any of your courtiers could take the lion out of the cage without breaking the cage or changing the lion's posture". All were puzzled. No one was able to do it. All were waiting for Birbal who had gone on a pilgrimage. He was expected to return in a month. The time given to solve the problem was only twenty days. Akbar was worried.

Next day, Abdul Fazal and Fawzi offered to bring the lion out of the cage after breaking its body. It was not possible. The lion's body was made out of some metal.

Luckily, Birbal came back early as his wife could not bear the heat during the journey. Akbar sent for him immediately and showed the cage to him. Birbal examined the cage and lion carefully and asked for a day to solve the problem. Akbar was confident that Birbal would be able to solve it. Birbal found that the lion was made out of wax and was given a coating of metal.

Next day, he brought an iron rod. When he came to the court, Birbal asked his attendant to heat the rod until it became red hot. The rod had a wooden handle. Birbal took the red-hot rod near the lion. The lion started melting in the heat. In a few minutes, the whole body was melted.

Then, there was no lion in the cage. The puzzle was solved. Akbar was very happy. All the courtiers admired Birbal.

❑

65.

Akbar and His Empress

One day, Akbar got angry with his empress and ordered her to leave his palace immediately.

The empress tried to speak, but Akbar would not listen. “Go away. You may, however, take with you, whatever is dear to you but leave my palace now”.

The empress was very upset and did not know what to do. Then she thought of Birbal and had him called. When Birbal came, she told him all that had happened.

Birbal said, "The emperor said that you could take what was dear to you. Is that right, Your Highness?"

"Yes," said the empress.

Birbal told his plan to the empress and went away. The empress told her maids to pack her clothes.

When the packing was done, she asked her maid to tell Akbar to come and meet her as she was going. Akbar came and stood silently. He was still angry and would not speak with her.

The empress said, "Don't talk if you don't want to but have this juice".

Birbal had asked the empress to put a sleeping pill in the juice. Akbar felt drowsy after drinking it and fell asleep.

Birbal had planned everything already. The sleeping emperor was carefully carried to a palanquin.

With the sleeping emperor in the palanquin, the empress left with her bodyguards for her father's house.

When they reached her father's house, he was very surprised but glad to have them come to stay with him. Akbar was carried to a room and laid on a bed.

Her father was worried to see the sleeping Akbar being carried to bed, but the empress said, "Don't worry, father. He will wake up in an hour".

When Akbar woke up, he was shocked to see where he was. Angrily, he shouted at his wife, who was standing nearby, "How did I come here?"

The empress said, "Don't be angry, Your Majesty, I was just obeying your orders".

Akbar said, "What do you mean?"

His wife said, "When you asked me to leave the palace, you had said that I could take with me whatever was dear to me. Well, you are the dearest of all to me, so I brought you with me".

Forgetting his anger, Akbar burst out laughing.

He said, "You are very clever, my dear wife".

"No. This was Birbal's clever thinking," confessed the empress.

Akbar said, "Birbal! I should have known. We are so lucky to have him. His clever thinking got us together. God bless him."

❑

66.

The Obedient Husbands

One day, Akbar and Birbal were roaming the streets of Agra, dressed like common men. Akbar would often roam the streets in a disguise to see if the people in his kingdom were happy or not and if they had any problems.

As they were walking along, they heard a woman shouting at her husband, "You are good for nothing. Go away and come back only when you have proved your worth".

Akbar and Birbal saw that the wife was short and thin but the husband was tall and strong. Yet, the husband was quietly listening to his wife's scolding.

Akbar asked, "Why doesn't the husband shout back at his wife?"

Birbal said, "The husband has to listen without shouting back. This is nothing new, My Lord. Please believe me. Every husband listens to his wife. This is the real truth of marriage".

The next day when the courtiers came into the court, Akbar told them, "All the married men come in front and all those, who are not married, stay behind".

All the married men stepped forward.

Akbar then said, "All right. Now all the husbands who listen to their wives should step to my right. Those who don't obey their wives should step to my left".

Akbar was shocked when all, but one man moved towards their right. It meant that Birbal was right.

Akbar said, "Birbal, you were wrong".

Birbal replied, "Your Majesty, let me first ask this man a question. Why did you not join the others?"

"Sir, I was about to go with the others and then I remembered that my wife had told me not to go with the crowd. So, I stay away from the crowd".

Everyone burst out laughing and Akbar said, "So you listen to your wife too. All right, I believe you, Birbal. You have again proved that you are right. All husbands do listen to their wives".

❑

67.

Blind Eyes

The empress came to her husband, Emperor Akbar and said, "My Lord, I want to donate charity to every blind person in the city".

Akbar ordered for a list of all the blind men in the city to be made. The list was prepared within a day and given to Akbar,

Akbar said, "I think the courtiers could prepare the list so soon because there are very few blind people in our city".

Birbal said, "But, Your Majesty, I have to say one thing. More than the blind people, many people have eyesight, yet cannot see".

Akbar did not believe him, so Birbal said, "I will prove myself right in a few days".

After some days, Birbal sat on the roadside stringing jute ropes on a cot.

Two men, passing by, asked him, "What are you doing, Birbal?"

Birbal had a clerk standing next to him, He said, "Start writing one, two".

The clerk wrote as asked. As Birbal continued stringing the cot, more people asked, "What are you doing?" And Birbal continued his counting, "Eighty-one, eighty-two, eighty-three".

Soon this news reached the palace and Akbar too came to see for himself, what Birbal was up to.

Akbar saw Birbal stringing the cot.

He could not understand why Birbal was doing this, so he also asked, "Birbal, what are you doing?"

Birbal did not look at Akbar. He went on stringing the cot and spoke out, "Two hundred and fifty".

Birbal stopped stringing the cot and took the paper with the numbers from the clerk and gave it to

Akbar saying, "Your Highness, I had promised that I will give you the list of people who had eyes but could not see. Here are two hundred and fifty names of such people. Please see it. Each of these people could see me stringing the jute in broad daylight, yet asked me what I was doing".

Akbar said "That is good. I am convinced now. Let me see the list".

Akbar went through the list as everyone stood silently. Then Akbar suddenly shouted, "Birbal, why have you written my name here?"

Birbal smiled and said, "Your Majesty. You were the last one to come and ask me what I was doing".

Akbar laughed saying, "Very true, Birbal. I did ask you that question".

❑

68.

The Gifts of God

One day when Birbal came late to the court, everyone turned towards him and started laughing. He could make out that they had been making fun of him.

Akbar said, “Birbal, we were discussing that all of us are fair, then why is it that you have darker skin?”

Birbal replied, “That’s true, My Lord. There is a secret behind this which no one knows”.

Then Akbar said angrily "Birbal, have you kept a secret from me, even you, emperor? I order you to tell it to me".

Birbal replied politely, "I will do as you say, Your Majesty. I will have to tell you about something from the past".

Akbar said, "Tell us. We want to know". All the courtiers agreed.

Then Birbal explained, "God created the world. God felt something was amiss, so he made plants, birds, and animals".

Akbar said, "That is no secret".

Birbal said, "But still God was not happy, so God made the man. Then He felt happy and thought of bestowing gifts upon all of us".

Akbar asked, "What gifts, Birbal?"

Birbal replied, "God threw money, looks, and brains down on the earth. He gave five minutes to all to pick up as many gifts as they could".

Then Akbar asked, "So? What happened then?"

"My secret is that I spent all the five minutes in gathering wit and cleverness, and did not have time for the other two. But all of you were busy picking up looks and money. This is my secret".

Many courtiers felt bad because they knew that Birbal had in a way said that they were not clever. But Akbar laughed loudly, appreciating Birbal's clever reply.

❑

69.

The Daughter of Birbal

One day, Birbal's daughter asked her father to take her to the court of Akbar. She was very young and wanted to see the palace of Akbar.

Birbal took her to the palace and then she went around all the gardens and saw all the rooms of the palace.

She lived in a big house herself because her father, Birbal was a minister in Akbar's court, but she found that everything was grander and more beautiful in Akbar's huge palace.

When she had seen everything, she was taken to the court of Akbar.

Birbal introduced her to Akbar. On Akbar's orders, she was given wonderful things to eat and drink.

Then Akbar started talking to her. He asked, "Did you like my palace?"

She just nodded her head.

Akbar picked her up and made her sit on his lap. Then he asked, "Do you know how to talk?"

She nodded and said, "Yes, Your Majesty. Neither less nor more".

Akbar asked, "What do you mean?"

She replied, "I talk less with elders and more with my friends".

Akbar laughed and said, "Birbal, your daughter has given such a quick reply. She is just like you, clever and witty".

❑

70.

A Hair of Moustache

Akbar was getting ready for the court. As he was being dressed, his grandson came running to him.

Akbar's grandson sat on his lap and said, "There is something on your moustache. Bend down, grandpa and I will remove it". Akbar bent down, and Khurram pulled one hair from his white moustache.

Akbar shouted, "Ooooh! You naughty boy! What have you done?"

Khurram ran away shouting, "See grandpa, I have fooled you".

Akbar walked to his court and thought, “I must put this question to my courtiers and see what they answer. Oh, I will enjoy myself! This time even Birbal will not be able to answer”.

Akbar then questioned his courtiers, “Someone pulled out one hair from my moustache. I want you all to guess his name and tell me what kind of punishment should be given to that person”.

The courtiers were unable to guess the person’s name. They wondered as to who could have dared to pull a hair from their emperor’s moustache?

One courtier shouted, “Whosoever it may be, that person should be jailed”.

Another courtier said, “Put him under an elephant’s legs”.

Others shouted, “Hang him, My Lord”.

Akbar was very happy that no one had been able to guess the culprit’s name.

Akbar saw that Birbal was very quiet. Akbar thought, “Well, this time even Birbal does not know the answer, that is why he is not answering”.

Akbar said, “Birbal, why have you not yet suggested any punishment?”

“I think, Your Majesty, you should give that person a kiss,” Birbal said confidently.

Akbar thought, "This answer shows that Birbal has understood who pulled my moustache hair. He is very clever. I can never defeat him". But the other courtiers were shocked.

"What are you saying?" asked one.

"Are you out of your mind?" said another.

Akbar asked, "A kiss is given as a reward, not as a punishment, Birbal. Why do you want me to reward and not punish the culprit?"

Birbal said, "Your Highness, you don't need to give any punishment. No one can dare to pull out the hair of your moustache because you are the king".

"But I am telling the truth, someone has done that, "Akbar insisted.

Birbal said, "Yes, I know that, Your Majesty. But I think that only a child could have had done it. And that also your grandson whom you love so much. So, you should kiss him".

Akbar said, "You are right again, Birbal. It was Khurram who playfully pulled the hair from my moustache."

❑

71.

A Chariot for Birbal

Akbar was very busy in the court when a messenger came and said, "My Lord, the Queen wants you to meet her now".

Akbar said, "Tell her that I am busy".

After some time, the messenger came again and said, "Your Highness, the Queen wants you to meet her at once".

Akbar got off the throne to go to his wife. As he was going, he saw Birbal smile, which annoyed him.

Akbar shouted at Birbal, “This smile is an insult to me. How dare you make fun of me, Birbal! You must be punished for this”.

Birbal stood up as Akbar ordered, “Go away from here at once, and never put your foot on this ground”.

Birbal walked out and went home. For many days, no one saw Birbal in the court. They didn’t see him anywhere. Even Akbar began missing Birbal, for he always made him laugh.

One day, Akbar was standing by the window when he saw Birbal on a chariot. He shouted to a servant, “Go and call Birbal at once”.

The servant ran outside. Birbal did not come inside but brought his chariot near the window where Akbar was standing.

Akbar pretended to be angry and said, “Birbal, why are you here? I told you not to put your foot here again”.

Birbal said, “I am following your orders, Your Majesty”.

“I told you to go but you have come back. You did not obey me,” said Akbar.

Birbal said, “My Lord, you had said that I should not put my foot on your ground ever again. I am obeying you”.

"But you are in the city," said Akbar.

"I am on a chariot, Your Majesty and not on the ground," said Birbal.

"So what?" asked Akbar.

Birbal said, "Your Majesty,' ground' also means soil. So I went to the next kingdom and got soil from there".

"Why?" asked Akbar.

Birbal said, "I spread the soil of the other kingdom on the floor of the chariot. Now my feet rest on, the soil of another kingdom and not your empire".

Akbar asked, "And when you get off?"

Birbal said, "I don't get off this chariot at all. I live on this chariot. Because I don't want to leave your kingdom and go anywhere. On the chariot, I will be in your kingdom but not on your ground".

Akbar said, "Your answer has touched me, Birbal. I take back my words. I forgive you. Now you need not stay on a chariot. Come down".

So with the clever-wit, Birbal back and the court was full of life again.

❑

72.

The Mother Tongue

A stranger was brought to the court. He bowed in front of Akbar and very politely said, “My respects to you”.

Akbar asked, “Who are you and where do you come from?”

The stranger replied, “My Lord, I am a master of many languages like Arabic, Persian and Sanskrit”.

He continued, “I have heard that in your court, there are many clever and learned people. I want them to tell you where I am from”.

Akbar said, "But how will they know where you are from?"

The man said, "From the way a person speaks, others can make out the place one belongs to. Can anyone here guess the place I belong to?"

Akbar said, "Yes, of course. Many people in my kingdom are wise and will be able to find out. Meanwhile, be my guest and stay in the palace".

Akbar ordered the learned people of his kingdom to find out where the man was from. These people talked for a long time with the stranger.

Then one of them said to Akbar, "Your Majesty, he speaks many languages so fluently that we cannot make out the place he belongs to".

Akbar then turned to Birbal and said, "Do you have anything to say, Birbal".

Akbar continued, "Can't you find out, Birbal?"

Birbal replied confidently, "I will tell you tomorrow morning, Your Majesty".

As planned, at night, Birbal's loyal servant quietly entered the room where the stranger was sleeping. He splashed some water on the sleeping man's face.

The man got up with a start, speaking loudly.

Birbal, who had been hiding in the room all this while, heard the stranger speak and quietly left the room.

Next day in the court, Akbar looked at Birbal hopefully.

Akbar asked, "Birbal, could you find out where this man comes from?"

Birbal said, "Yes, My Lord, I am sure that he is from Gujarat".

The surprised stranger said, "That is true but how did you find out?"

Birbal smiled and said, "When a person is angry, in pain or surprise, he will always talk in his mother tongue. Last night, while you were sleeping, my servant sprinkled some water on you and you got up suddenly, shouting in Gujarati".

The stranger turned to Birbal and said, "That was very clever. You are truly wise and intelligent, Birbal".

Everyone nodded with a smile, agreeing with the stranger.

Akbar said, "Birbal, I am happy that you have kept the honour of our kingdom".

❑

73.

A Step to Death

Akbar was coming down the stairs of the library with Birbal. There were too many steps and Akbar was feeling bored.

Akbar said, "Birbal, do you see these steps? It is a long way down. Now Birbal, you have to do one thing for me".

Birbal replied, "Yes, Your Majesty".

Akbar said, "Well, I am your emperor and so you have to obey me. By the time we reach the last step, you should be able to make me laugh. If you don't, then you will be punished to death".

Birbal had no choice but to obey. Birbal was not worried because he knew he could make Akbar laugh quite easily.

So he walked down the stairs with Emperor Akbar and started telling him a joke. But Akbar just did not laugh.

Birbal began to narrate another joke, then another, but Akbar would not laugh.

Birbal was not worried because there were yet many steps to go and he was sure that he would make Akbar laugh.

Birbal told many other jokes but it seemed that Akbar had made up his mind not to laugh at all. He would not even smile. Birbal then made funny faces but Akbar remained serious.

Now Birbal was really worried. They had come down the stairs and only a few steps remained.

Birbal counted and found that there were ten steps left.

He quickly thought of other jokes but none would come to his mind. Then he just began making up his jokes.

But Emperor Akbar was not amused. Birbal started feeling afraid because he knew that emperors could get people hanged easily. Sometimes even just because they were angry or upset.

Birbal started trembling as only five steps were left.

Now four steps were left. No jokes seemed to come to his mind. Just three steps were left. Birbal tried to tell a joke, but couldn't because he was really afraid now. So he kept silent.

They stepped on the second last step.

Birbal realized that his end was near because he couldn't make Akbar laugh.

They were on the last step and Birbal could see his death very clearly now.

Out of fear, Birbal screamed at the emperor, "You rogue. Why don't you laugh? Will you laugh only after you get me hanged?"

No one could speak so rudely to the emperor. Birbal thought that now he would be surely punished to death.

But after hearing Birbal calling him a rogue and seeing his scared face, Akbar burst out laughing and went on laughing as he stepped down to the bottom of the stairs. Birbal was relieved.

Birbal apologized to his king but he realized that Akbar's timely laughter had saved him from certain death.

❑

74.

Shorten the Road

Emperor Akbar was travelling to a distant place along with some of his courtiers. It was a hot day and the emperor was tired with the journey.

"Can't anybody shorten this road for me?" he asked, querulously.

"I can," said Birbal.

The other courtiers looked at one another, perplexed. All of them knew there was no other path through the hilly terrain.

The road they were travelling on was the only one that could take them to their destination.

"You can shorten the road?" said the emperor. "Well, do it".

"I will," said Birbal. "Listen first to this story I have to tell".

And riding beside the emperor's palanquin, he launched upon a long and intriguing tale that held Akbar and all those listening, spellbound. Before they knew it, they had reached the end of their journey.

"We've reached?" exclaimed Akbar. "So soon!"

"Well," grinned Birbal. "You did say you wanted the road to be shortened".

❑